Part Ten

To Prevent Open Minds

Emily Martha Sorensen

Also by Emily Martha Sorensen

Wicked Witches of Restva:
Black Magic Academy
White Magic Academy

The End in the Beginning:
The Keeper and the Rulership
The Fires of the Rulership
The Magic or the Rulership

Fairy Senses:
Fairy Eyeglasses
Fairy Compass
Fairy Earmuffs
Fairy Barometer
Fairy Pox
Fairy Slippers
Fairy Lunchbox
Fairy Icepack
Fairy Stopwatch
Fairy Toothbrush
Fairy Perfume
Fairy Crown

Dragon Eggs:
Dragon's Egg
Dragon's Hope
Dragon's First Christmas
Dragon's Fire
Dragon's Song
Dragon's First Valentine

Comics:
A Magical Roommate
To Prevent World Peace

The Numbers Just Keep
Getting Bigger:
Twenty-Four Potential
Children of Prophecy

Trilogy of a Teenage Werevulture:
Trials of a Teenage Werevulture
Trifles of a Teenage Werevulture

Weredodo Cozy Mysteries:
Weredodo Sleuth

Not Quite a Harem:
Not Quite a Curse

Magical Mayhem:
To Prevent World Peace
To Prevent Chic Costumes
To Prevent Clear Paths
To Prevent Smart Choices
To Prevent Warm Welcomes
To Prevent Cute Mascots
To Prevent First Place (prologue)
To Prevent Fresh Starts
To Prevent New Allies
To Prevent Best Friends

Short Story Collections:
Worlds of Wonder
Magic and Mischief
Tales of Tie-Ins

Picture Books:
Tabby, Tabby, Burning Bright

To Prevent Open Minds

Magical Mayhem Part #10: To Prevent Open Minds
Copyright © 2019 by Emily Martha Sorensen
Cover and internal art by Emily Martha Sorensen

ISBN: 978-1-949607-61-1

http://www.emilymarthasorensen.com

To Frederik Vendelin,

longtime fan of the comic,
reader of my other books,
and Patreon supporter.

Chapter 1
The Agenda

Light faded and then reappeared as sparkles twinkled around the two of them.

So that's what teleportation feels like, Florence thought. It wasn't the way she'd expected. She'd thought it would make her unsettled and nauseous, but there was no sense of disorientation; it was just clear that her surroundings were different.

Florence looked around, taking in those surroundings. She was now in what looked like a very rich house, with a sweeping staircase leading up to a grand entryway. There was almost nothing in the way of furniture to fill the cavernous space, but there were posters of cuddly animals plastered all over the walls, and, oddly, several cannons lined up by the top of the stairs.

On the only piece of furniture in this room, a comfy-looking armchair, a woman with stringy hair sat dozing with her head on her chest. She had a messy granny square on her lap that looked like someone who knew nothing about crocheting had done it.

"Soothsayer!" Kendra said loudly. "I brought you a visitor!"

The woman's head snapped up, and she jumped at the sight before her. "Kendra! What on *Earth?!*"

"Hello, oracle. This is Florence." Kendra gestured over at her best friend and yanked the watch out of her grasp. "You're now going to show her everything you showed me."

"You mean the future you *prevented?*" the woman asked with intense annoyance. "Which now no longer *exists?*"

"Yes. Show her that one."

"I can't show people futures that no longer exist, Kendra!"

"That's a stupid limitation on your power," Kendra snorted. "It would be so much better if you were a magical girl. Then you could power up and change that."

"Yes, thank you, I appreciate your rubbing that in," the woman said tightly.

"So, you're the . . . born mage who showed Kendra her future originally?" Florence ventured.

The woman glanced over at her. A lock of stray, greasy hair fell into her face, and she didn't bother to move it. "Yes. And you're her best friend, Florence Atkins, also known as Pink Dragon, also known as Crimson Dragon, also known as the new leader of the Magical Girl Union. Thank you so much for that."

Florence swallowed. She hadn't expected to be brought before someone this . . . this carelessly untidy. All the villains she'd ever met had been well-dressed, well-groomed, and smooth in their cunning words.

"And you're a villain," Florence said cautiously. "Why should I trust a word you say?"

The woman slammed her fist on her knee. "I am not a villain!"

"You work with Kendra, don't you?" Florence glanced over at her best friend.

Kendra smirked.

"Not by choice," the woman said grumpily. "Your best friend bullied me into it. She's exceptionally good at being annoying."

Kendra smirked wider.

That gave Florence pause. She'd always assumed the born mage had recruited Kendra. Had it actually been the opposite?

"But you're a villain now," she said. "Because you work with Kendra."

The woman pursed her lips and looked sour.

"Right, we're villains saving the world," Kendra said briskly. "Now show Florence that future, and I'll take her home."

"I *just* explained to you —!"

"Just show her something," Kendra interrupted.

The woman sighed and rolled her eyes. "See what I have to put up with?" she complained. "My name is Chronos, by the way. Not 'oracle.' Not 'soothsayer.'"

"Try picking a cool villain name, and I'll call you that instead," Kendra said idly.

"I *did!* My name is *Chronos!*"

"I said a *cool* villain name."

"Wait. Hang on a second," Chronos said slowly. "Why are all of Tiffany's futures currently in England?"

"I left her there," Kendra said casually.

"You *left her there?!*"

"She sided with the magical girl thief," Kendra snapped. "She deserves to learn a lesson about betraying her teammate."

"What makes you think she's going to learn a lesson from this?! If she stays there any longer, she's going to try to team up with Robbin' Red Riding Hood! And in some futures, she might even succeed!"

"Hmph!" Kendra got that stuck-up, pigheaded look on her face that said, *I'm not going to admit I made a mistake.*

Florence raised a pointer finger cautiously. "Is there any chance I can see this future I'm supposed to see, so I can go home?"

"Yes," Chronos said, eyeing Kendra. "Just as soon as Tiffany's back here."

"Ha!" Kendra said with eloquent scorn.

"Kendra," Chronos said through clenched teeth, "you don't get to abandon your teammate in a foreign country."

"She's not a teammate. She betrayed me. Show the future."

"First *you* go back to England and get Tiffany!"

"*Hmph!*" Kendra spun around to turn her back on both of them. "I'm sure she'll be fine on her own."

"Regardless of that being *true* . . ." Chronos folded her arms. "Get. Tiffany. Now."

Kendra didn't budge an inch. "Show. Future. First."

"Uh . . . how many teammates do you have?" Florence asked.

"One," Kendra said, pointing at Chronos.

"*Two!*" the born mage shouted.

Florence put a hand to her forehead. "I don't know any of this situation. Would someone please explain what's going on here?"

Kendra gestured at the messy woman. "Born mage. Sees the future. Showed me mine. Why I defected."

"Yes . . . I understand that. But this Tiffany girl . . ."

"I should've known she couldn't be trusted," Kendra groused. "She was raised by villains."

"So . . . you shouldn't have trusted her because she was raised by villains. And . . . you chose to trust a born mage because . . .?"

"Because she was right, duh. It didn't matter that she was a villain."

"I can hear EVERY WORD YOU'RE SAYING!" Chronos yelled. "Born mages are *not* all evil! Most of us are just *ordinary people* who are persecuted because we happen to have magic —"

"Yada yada yada," Kendra interrupted. "Would you just show Florence the future already?"

"After you get Tiffany!"

"Oh, no. You're going to show her the future first."

"I am not! You're going to get Tiffany first!"

"You know . . . there's such a thing as compromise," Florence suggested.

They both looked at her.

"I mean, both things could happen at the same time."

There was a long silence.

"All right. We'll compromise," Chronos said abruptly. "I'll show her the future . . . *while* you go and get Tiffany."

"Fine." Kendra spun around and stalked off. "But you had better convince her."

Then she disappeared in a stream of sparkles.

Florence drew in a deep breath, looking at the stranger she was now alone with. So this was a born mage, like Lute Deathwave?

The woman's eyes were weird. She seemed to have no pupils. And yet, despite that being necessary for sight, she acted like she could see just fine.

Chronos didn't break the awkward silence. It just stretched on and on and on.

"Um . . . hi," Florence said at last.

"Hello. I'm Chronos." The woman walked back to her chair and flopped down in it. "I've seen you in a lot of futures."

"Have you?"

"Mm-hm. I've been watching Kendra for a long time, and you were always in her futures."

Of course I was. Florence took a deep breath. "Why did you tell her to turn villain? Why did you tell her it was the only way to prevent the bad future you showed her?"

"I didn't. I told her not to turn evil. I'm not sure she completely grasped the concept."

Florence let out a spurt of laughter.

"I'm neutral," Chronos said. "I always have been."

Quickly sobering, Florence shook her head. "There's no such thing. Not taking sides means supporting evil by default."

"Oh, believe me, I could support evil for real if I wanted to." Making a face, Chronos rummaged around beneath her, and finally pulled a crochet hook out from under her rear. "I don't."

Florence took a deep breath. "So what's my future that Kendra is so concerned about?"

"Obviously it's not your future she cares about. She told me to convince you."

"Um . . . convince me of what . . .?"

"To give up what you're doing, I guess. She wants you to see the future of your precious Union." The born mage woman cracked her knuckles. "Do you want to see it?"

Florence gulped and nodded.

"You! You again! Stop helping me! Stop following me!" the red-haired eleven-year-old shrieked, catching sight of her stalker. "You're making everything worse!"

Tiffany ignored this poor repayment for her good work.

"I made it easier for you to break in tonight!" she said proudly.

The girl who transformed into Robbin' Red Riding Hood had a horrified look on her face. "Oh, no. What've you done *now?*"

"I used my BREAK IT! power on the walls —"

"You broke the walls?!"

"Yes, but then a bunch of magical girls showed up and fixed them —"

"Well, obviously! That's why thieves are subtle!"

"But first I left a note so that you didn't have to!" Tiffany said excitedly. "I said you'd be coming at 3:25 in the morning —"

"3:25?!" The red-haired girl looked faintly hysterical. "I have to go at 3:25?!"

"Uh huh!" Tiffany beamed. "Oh, but we can be sneaky. We can show up at 3:20 instead. They'll never expect it."

The red-haired girl moaned. "I didn't want to give them an exact time! Now if I don't show up, Mysterious Mystery Detective Cute will brag that she scared me off! Thanks a lot."

"You're welcome!" Tiffany beamed. "Tonight, I'll help you by breaking the walls again —"

"STOP HELPING! You're the reason I couldn't get into the museum a single time last night!"

Tiffany giggled. "Well, it was funny to watch the detective magical girl run after you. She's cool, too!"

The bell to the school behind them rang.

"Lunch is over! I have to go back to school!" the red-headed girl said frantically. "Don't do anything else, you hear? Don't leave any notes. Don't break anything. Just hide up a tree!"

Tiffany pouted. "But I'm really, really hungry."

"Well, you can't have *my* lunch! I already ate it! Just hide somewhere, okay?" The red-haired girl ran away.

Tiffany climbed up a tree and sat there, swinging her legs.

Down below, she saw a pair of boys her age walking past, opening up a package of something that said "digestive biscuits." But instead of biscuits inside, there were what looked like —

"Cookies!" Tiffany squealed quietly.

She should ask them to share!

Oh, but what if they wouldn't share?

She could steal them! Yes, that was the perfect idea!

Oh, wait . . . Tiffany remembered dimly. *Chronos says I shouldn't steal things because it's wrong . . .*

But then again, the man she had called "Daddy," the villain who'd raised her, had once explained to her that when people told you something was wrong, you just had to figure out why it was actually right. It was called "rationalization."

Tiffany put a finger to her mouth. *They have cookies, therefore they're rich. I am hungry, therefore I'm poor. Robbin' Red Riding Hood robs the rich to feed the poor. Robbin' Red Riding Hood is cool. Being cool equals being right. Therefore, Robbin' Red Riding Hood is right.*

That logic seemed sound!

Yaaaaaaaay! Tiffany thought gleefully, summoning her wand. *Robbin' Red Riding Hood would be so proud of me!*

Then a hand seized the back of her cape.

"Hi, Tiffany," Kendra said in an unfriendly voice. "Chronos wants you returned to the lair."

"Noooo!" Tiffany wailed. "I'm supposed to get cookies!"

But it was too late. They vanished from the tree in a shower of sparkles.

It wasn't just one future Chronos showed her. It was dozens. Dozens and dozens of possible futures, all of them bad.

And first, Florence was on the verge of panic, leaning forward with her fingernails digging into her palms. But after the third one . . . she started to question.

There was something missing from all of them.

"Here's another one of the possible futures," Chronos said, holding her hands apart so that the scene was easy to see. "Your new supporter, Dulcina, becomes a problem. In some of the futures, she splits off to found her own organization about magical girl superiority. Here's one where her success leads to a war across the magical girl community."

A vicious and bloodless battlefield.

"Here's one where, if she fails, fanatic followers sabotage Moon Base."

The moon exploded across the sky.

"Here's one where the Russian tsar is assassinated."

A terrifying and gory battlefield.

"Here's one with the Japanese emperor."

Pure chaos across Japan.

Florence said nothing.

"Now for a different kind of danger," Chronos said. "Suppose Eloise Santos loses the next election? Here's a replacement president who could be a disaster: Francisco Delgado, an outright warmonger. Watch how the Union would change under his leadership."

She displayed a man with short hair and a tiny, long braid standing behind the podium at a Magical Girl Union meeting, shouting spiels that had hundreds of girls in costumes cheering.

Florence said nothing.

Not seeming to notice her silence, Chronos kept going.

"Here's one where villains infiltrate the Union."

"Here's one where Snowbelle's magical girl form is killed."

"Here's one where mismanagement of funds by twelve-year-old 'accountants' leads to a huge scandal."

"Here's one where a hostile nation annexes Mágico."

"Here's one where *you* get assassinated."

"I don't buy it," Florence broke in.

Chronos blinked. "What?"

"I don't buy it. There's something crucial missing from every future you've shown me."

Chronos looked baffled. "No, there isn't. I've been showing you every—"

"Hope." Florence folded her arms. "You haven't shown me one future with hope. Twenty-seven futures, and not one of them is positive? That's implausible, at best. Lying, at worst. You clearly have an agenda. Even if you're just exaggerating to try to convince me, that doesn't quite engender my trust. I came to see my futures, and I think you're leaving out half of them."

Chronos's eyes widened. "I never said there were *no* positive futures! There are plenty of those. Of course! It's just that the risks are high enough that if things go wrong, there's a high likelihood it will —"

"Forgive me, but there are always risks," Florence said. She got to her feet. "And I'm not going to let my fear — *or yours* — stop me."

Chronos stared at her, mute.

"If those futures you showed me are genuine and not just some illusion power, I thank you for bringing them to my attention," Florence said firmly. "But in the meantime . . ."

She turned and started to walk away.

Then she stopped abruptly.

"Er . . . how do I get home from here?" she asked awkwardly.

Chronos's shoulders slumped. "Kendra will take you."

"Oh, no, I won't," Kendra said, teleporting into the room.

"Kendra!" Chronos exclaimed. "Were you eavesdropping?!"

"Duh. I've been sitting in the plotting room behind you for half an hour."

"It was a private conversation!"

"It was an *informative* conversation. Anyway, I'm not taking Florence anywhere."

"Er . . . why not?" Florence asked cautiously.

Kendra jabbed her finger to emphasize every word. "Because you're going to stay here until you *listen!*"

"I *did* listen!" Florence snapped. "She said there are risks. Okay! There are risks! I'll try to avoid them!"

"You can avoid all of them by dissolving the Union!"

"I'm not going to do that, Kendra!"

"Well, I'm not taking you home until you agree to!"

"Just because I don't agree with your conclusions doesn't mean you have the right to take me hostage!"

"Nobody's taking anybody hostage!" Chronos sounded alarmed. "The last thing I need is more freeloaders living —"

"You think you listened? You're going to stay here until you *understand,* then!" Kendra bellowed.

"Understand what?" Florence asked acidly. "That you were so scared of some possible future that you jettisoned your whole life to prevent it? I *don't* understand that, Kendra!"

"It was *necessary!*" Kendra shouted.

"No, it was stupid, overreactive, and *insane!*"

"Fine!" Kendra spun around, breathing heavily. "Go home, then. Find a way by yourself. See if I care."

Florence put a hand to her forehead. Her best friend was so impossible. "But . . . I can't just teleport. I still need you to take me . . ."

Kendra let out a wordless scoff that expressed how she felt about that idea.

"Did you bring Tiffany home?" Chronos asked with an edge in her voice.

"Of course," Kendra said, waving her hand contemptuously. "I left her in the kitchen. She said she was hungry."

"TIFFANY!" Chronos called, raising her voice. "I have a present for you!"

There was a scramble of footsteps, and a girl who looked about ten with blonde pigtails exploded out of a room off to the side. "A present? Ooh! What?!"

Florence stared. *This* was Kendra's other teammate? The one who'd betrayed her and earned Kendra's ire? A little girl?

Chronos had a gleam in her eyes. "I'm going to let you use the watch for a few hours."

"OOH!" Tiffany squealed. "I can't wait to play with Wallie!"

Kendra's jaw dropped. "You can't do that! It's mine!"

"Funny how I don't care."

"Funny how she can't possibly get it off me," Kendra snarled, putting her hand over the watch on her wrist.

"Tiffany," Chronos said, "you have my permission to break the watch."

"Okay!" Tiffany summoned her wand.

Kendra vanished in a shower of sparkles.

Florence was getting the distinct impression that she wasn't going to be getting home anytime soon.

Kendra reappeared across the room.

Her spiked halo was now pressed against the back of Tiffany's neck, her other arm squeezed across the girl's chest, keeping her from moving her arms or escaping.

"Okay, I won't break Wallie, promise!" Tiffany yelped.

"You wouldn't kill her," Chronos said quickly, looking alarmed.

"Wouldn't I?"

"You don't kill human lives. Just magical girl forms."

Kendra's eyes were dark. "You can't see the past, so you don't know. Florence, have I killed people before?"

Florence winced. "Yes."

"Who were the people I killed?"

"Villains."

"Is she a hero or a villain?"

Florence's voice was hoarse. "I guess a . . . villain."

"You wouldn't do that." Chronos looked unsure of those words. "Not with someone you know."

Kendra looked at her best friend with steady eyes. "Have I ever tried to kill someone I knew well?"

Florence felt like crying. ". . . Yes. You tried to kill my boyfriend after he betrayed us."

"Yes. I did." The spiked halo disappeared from Kendra's hand, and she stepped away from the ten-year-old. "But my future isn't to become Avenging Angel anymore."

The pigtailed girl yelped and dashed up the stairs.

Everyone was silent for a long moment.

"Is that why you believed her?" Florence asked quietly.

"Yes." Kendra's eyes were dark. "Because I knew it was true. I knew I was capable of what she was showing me. That's why I had to be a villain. It was the only way to make sure I wouldn't go down that path anyway. It was the only way to make sure nobody could wreck the world in my name."

Florence drew in a breath. "I promise," she said. "I *promise* I won't let the Union fall into any of those bad futures."

"How can you promise that?" Kendra demanded. "The same people are still there!"

"Because you have *her.*" Florence pointed at Chronos.

"Me?!" Chronos looked alarmed and wary.

"Yes." Florence nodded. "If all the futures go bad, Kendra, you can show up and kill the magical girl form of everyone who has no future of being innocent. Including me. As long as you do not attack for anything less, I won't stop you. And meanwhile, I'll do my best to make sure that never becomes necessary."

There was silence for a long moment.

"I think she *does* understand," Chronos said. "Take her home."

Kendra shot her an angry look.

"Or we could let Tiffany use the watch instead." Chronos folded her arms. "Hey, Tiffany, do you still want —?!"

"I'll do it! Just stop badgering me!" Kendra snarled.

"Awww . . . but I want my tuuuuuuuuurn!" Tiffany wailed from what she apparently thought was a safe distance upstairs.

Florence walked over and held out her hand.

Kendra took it.

"Then," Chronos added with a hint of asperity, "after you've done that, would you *please* get around to capturing Robbin' Red Riding Hood? She seems to have decided that the Koh-i-Noor diamond in the crown jewels will be an easier target because Tiffany won't be waiting to help her there, and she also thinks it would be a good idea to send that one to Egypt."

Chapter 2
The Plans

Greetings, minions!" Rhea said cheerfully, waving as she took a seat at the brand new table in the Olympian plotting room. "Welcome to this meeting! Good authority informs me that you four are the most reliable minions my family employs."

The plotting room was a pleasure to sit in, now that she had removed the appallingly bad furnishings from Great-Uncle Nico's tenure and replaced them with her own.

The carpet was black sable, no longer grey spotted with random bloodstains, the walls were freshly painted in glimmering silver and pearl, and the table itself was sleek ebony wood, carved with detailed nude figures from Greek mythology.

The bas relief in the center was her favorite detail. She had requested it particularly when ordering the commission. It showed the battle of Troy with Cassandra in the middle, weeping over the tragedy she had been helpless to prevent.

As a child, Rhea had often tormented her sister with that story, telling her that her fate was the fate of all born mages with the power to see the future . . . unless, of course, they teamed up with someone with a silver tongue.

Turning Chronos into a hopeless Cassandra, desperate enough to turn to her older sister at last, was exactly Rhea's goal here.

Of course, Rhea reflected, *whenever she does rejoin us here at Olympus Estates, I will have to have this table removed before she sees it and gets angry . . . but first things first.*

Rhea ran her manicured fingernails fondly across the table, reflecting upon how nice it was to have furniture without scratches from careless knives, holes from stray bullets, char from miniature explosions, and gouges from gratuitous spikes on costumes.

If anyone messed up her beautiful new furniture, she would of course have them killed.

Looking up from her ruminations, Rhea smiled. The minions at the table were all waiting in silence. They all knew better than to speak before she invited them to. It was so refreshing to not have to execute anyone to make an example about showing respect.

Rhea pointed at each one, naming them, a sign that they would now be allowed to speak freely.

"Urun, of the Danish syndicate."

The large-framed woman with sleepy eyes showed no emotion other than faint boredom. She wore an outfit that was bland grey, her hair was back in a conservative bun, and she wore no makeup and needed it. She overall gave off an impression of an extremely forgettable person.

That was, of course, how she had managed to wander around poor neighborhoods, pretending to be a new neighbor in order to recruit hundreds of people into a pyramid scheme selling gourmet chocolate that didn't really exist: by looking like a frumpy woman next door, nobody suspicious.

"Greybeard, the Disgruntled."

"Hmph!" that man responded, folding his arms. His hair and beard were well-kept, his eyebrows bushy, and he gave off an aura of permanent grumpiness.

He was fairly good at attacking magical girls, but his real skill was in escaping and being hard to chase. Rhea intended to use that in a much more lucrative way.

"Heracles, a member of the family."

"H-h-hello!" The boy hastily put away a book called *Villainy Made E-Z* that he'd been trying to read under the table.

Truthfully, Rhea had no idea whether he would be competent or not. He was the fourteen-year-old son of one of Rhea's most loyal supporters, who had insisted that his son would be a wonderful personal minion for her if she gave him a chance, so she'd felt obligated to offer the boy a position.

Still, the boy's power was mildly useful, and he was blindly loyal. He was one of those who believed that every word of the mythology about their ancestors was absolute truth, which made him zealously obedient to the current leader of the family.

It was laughable that anyone like that existed, but Rhea wasn't going to complain. People who were easy to manipulate were very entertaining.

Rhea looked over at the last of them, a man with his feet on the table. She would have scolded anyone else for that, or worse, but he knew he could get away with it without comment.

"And Drake."

Drake flicked a gaze over at her and gave her a lazy smile. He wasn't an Olympian minion at all, but rather an assassin Rhea was well-acquainted with and had hired a few times for her own purposes.

He was one of the many assassins Great-Uncle Nico had failed to pay promptly, so the only way Drake had agreed to come was when Rhea had promised to pay him four times what Great-Uncle Nico had owed him. He'd also demanded that the Olympians pay him up front for every job he did for them from now on.

Rhea had not only agreed, she'd paid him for his first two jobs up front before even setting up this meeting. He was a useful ally, and would be an undesirable enemy.

The fourteen-year-old with tidy hair raised his hand hesitantly. "You said, um, good authority informs you that we're the most competent. I'm sort of wondering . . . I mean, this is my first villain job. Ummm . . . so . . . exactly whose 'good authority' . . . ?"

"*Mine,*" Rhea said in an iron tone. "You *do* remember my power, don't you?"

Heracles gulped. He leaned over to Drake and whispered, "Psst . . . what is . . . ?"

"She sees the past, you idiot," Drake said, with no attempt to lower his voice.

"Which means I've vetted you all thoroughly, and personally." Rhea pressed her manicured fingernails against the table. "I know your strengths, your weaknesses, your hopes, your dreams, your suitability for any given job, and *every single one* of your secrets."

Heracles gulped and shrank back against his chair.

"Now for your first assignments," Rhea said, taking a sheet of paper from her lap and placing it on the table, face-down. "Drake, I have two targets for you to assassinate. You know who they are already. Greybeard, you'll deliver blackmail for me. Your ability to escape will come in handy when our repeat clients try to set traps to do away with you. Blackmail will be the family's main source of income for awhile, though we'll diversify as soon as it's convenient. Heracles, a mound of paperwork for you to go through. I assume you'll be well-suited to the task, given your power."

Heracles's face fell. It was clear he had been hoping for a role that was more exciting, but he wisely didn't complain.

His born mage ability was to be able to read anywhere from five hundred to two thousand words per minute with no loss of comprehension, which wasn't a great power in the grand scheme of things, but it could be helpful for the sake of efficiency.

"Urun, you'll be my shopgirl . . ."

"Excuse me?!" She looked outraged.

"My store's been closed for six weeks," Rhea said tartly. "I'm not going to let my business fall apart just because I'm now running the family. I need someone who can handle villain customers without letting them get away with anything, and who also looks unassuming enough to not make the regular clientele suspicious. You fit the description, though of course you'll need much better clothes and makeup than you are wearing currently."

Urun didn't seem flattered at all. "I don't want to work in retail! Give me a better job!"

Rhea's eyes narrowed. "The other job is to attack magical girls. What's your power again?"

She knew, of course.

"... Turning orange," Urun said in a surly voice.

"Well, if you want to leverage that into a combat ability, by all means ..."

"Wait!" Urun protested. "What about that minion you have already?! Zazz or something? She used to work as your shopgirl, right? Have her go back to that!"

"Minerva's far more valuable than you are," Rhea said crisply. "I have plans for her. Now, do you want to be my shopgirl or take a combat position for a ten percent dock in pay?"

"Fine, I'll do it," Urun muttered.

"Good." Rhea's smile didn't reach her eyes. "Now, Greybeard, you'll find your list of victims on this sheet of paper. There are two hundred to start blackmailing in the first month, since there are a lot we haven't started on yet. Right now, we're only going to go after the cash cows, but in a few months, we'll start pressuring the politicians again ..."

Zazz wandered into the boss's office, chomping on an apple. She wasn't hungry, but the opportunity to snack on the job was so sweet that she had to take advantage of it at every opportunity.

The boss's back was turned, and she seemed intent on something other than paperwork, for once. In fact, it looked like she was ... drawing?

Zazz swallowed her bite of apple. "Oh, hi, boss. What're you doing?"

"Hello, Minerva. Designing a costume for an infiltrator."

Does that mean we're going back to the fashion world? Zazz perked up. "Who're you infiltrating?"

"The Magical Girl Union."

Zazz paused. "Um ... Rhea ... I'm pretty sure one of those girls leading the Union has truth-telling powers."

Duh? she nearly added.

"Two, actually," Rhea said with an edge in her voice, standing up from the chair. It was clear she'd noticed the hint of rudeness. "Météore can tell if people are lying, and Xinghuo senses sincerity."

Zazz took a bite of her apple, not particularly concerned about the edge in her boss's tone. "So what's the point?"

"Oh, my dear Minerva." Rhea smirked. "Don't you know that reputations are everything?"

Zazz stared at her. "Huh?"

Rhea picked up the sketch from the table and looked at it fondly. "I'm going to be sending a minion around the world to spread the worst possible rumors in the worst possible places. We might not be able to stop the Union from existing, but we can erode its support and crumble it from within."

"Ha!" Zazz burst out laughing. "That's brilliant! But who are you going to make do it?"

Rhea turned and looked at her with a sly smile.

Ten minutes later, wearing a frilly pink dress, Zazz shouted, *"Why do you hate me?!"*

Rhea smirked, not the least bit deterred by this accusation. "You're a minion. Minions sometimes go undercover. Get used to it."

"You've made me look like a teenager! I don't want to look like a teenager! I'm twenty-two!"

"Fortunately, you don't look it."

"I won't do it! I won't! I *won't!*"

"Of course you'll be staying at the best hotels. I've booked you at the Waldorf Astoria in Berlin. You'll leave first thing tomorrow. Here are your first-class airline tickets."

"I *won't* —!"

"And a mobile phone to keep in contact with me." Rhea reached into a drawer and pulled out a bricklike thing that was the latest in conspicuous extravagance: a phone that didn't need to be plugged into a wall to work.

"Shiny new technology . . ." Zazz accepted the luxurious gift without thinking. Cellular phones were a brand new innovation, one she'd never held in her hands before. Something like this would be super, super useful for a traveling minion whose boss needed to keep them constantly updated —

"Wait! I'm not going to do it!"

"Oh, and feel free to use my Deathwave expense account for all shopping needs." Rhea turned and headed out of the room, waving casually. "I'm sure you'll need weapons, first-class accommodations, disguises, costumes, souvenirs, villain club memberships, flashy parties out with other minions . . ."

Obviously Zazz was being bribed, but it was hard to deny that the price was appealing.

Maybe I will . . .

Chapter 3
The Spy

Portuguese chatter flew across the improvised outdoor cafeteria, interspersed with jabbering in English and Spanish and occasionally other languages.

It was the midpoint break of the opening ceremonies of the Magical Girl Union, and free lunch was provided for all attendees, so nearly the entire audience was gathered in this open space and talking about their impressions so far.

At one table sat two girls who had just met in the lunch line, but were already talking like old friends.

"I'm Luciana," one of those girls introduced herself, picking up the spoon on her tray. *"Well, technically I'm Fitas e Laços, since I'm transformed right now."*

That name meant "Ribbons and Bows" in Portuguese, referring to the many ribbons and bows on her costume.

She picked up a bite of food and swallowed it.

The second girl watched her with fascination. *"I'm Emilia. When I'm transformed, my name's Elegancia, but I'm not transformed now. How are you doing that?"*

"Doing what?"

"Eating!"

Luciana was puzzled. *"I pick up a spoon, and . . ."*

"But you're transformed!"

"Ohhhhhh." Luciana put her spoon down, a little embarrassed. *"You just have to assume your magical girl form should be able to do those things the first time you transform, and it will be able to. I didn't do it on purpose; I guess it didn't make sense to me that I could have a body that didn't need to sleep and eat and use the bathroom. So, well, when I'm Fitas e Laços, I have to do all those things."*

Which made her pretty weak for a magical girl, all things considered. It wasn't exactly an advantage for your magical girl form to have human frailties and needs.

Breathing and aging were things most magical girl forms did, probably because those were so unconscious and constant that a girl would have to deliberately imagine them out before the first time she transformed in order to have them excluded. But things like being able to eat, sleep, or use the bathroom tended to only be present if a girl deliberately imagined them there.

For instance, Dulcina Caramelo could eat as a magical girl, but not sleep or use the bathroom. There was also a girl in Luciana's class, Dormilona, whose magical girl form could sleep, but not use the bathroom or eat.

Not wanting to talk about her unusual weakness of *needing* to eat, rather than merely having the ability to do so, Luciana said hastily, *"There are also other things I can do! For instance, I changed my hairstyle after transforming this morning."* She pointed to her side ponytail. *"When I transform, it's down."*

Emilia goggled. *"You can change your hairstyle?!"*

"Yep!" Luciana drew herself up proudly. *"I've been told it's a mild shapeshifting power. I can style my hair however I want, and it'll stay that way and never fall out. It just goes back to normal the next time I transform."*

"That's so amazing!" Emilia exclaimed. *"Most magical girl forms can't be altered at all! Except when powering up, I mean."*

Luciana was starting to feel proud of herself. *"That's not all. I also have a mild separation power. See?"*

She untied the ribbon from around her neck and handed it to the other girl.

Emilia gasped. *"Oh, my gosh! Are you sure you're transformed?"*

Luciana grinned. *"It's just a mild separation power. It only works on my costume. It's not as powerful as, say, Lentswe Counterpoint being able to split into two people."*

"She has a really cool power," Emilia said wistfully.

"Or this girl at school called Zombi who can take off her hands and send them somewhere else."

Emilia shuddered. *"Ew! That's so creepy!"*

"Excuse me!" a girl in a pink dress interrupted hopefully from behind them. She was holding a tray of food. *"Are you guys here for the opening ceremonies, too? Can I sit here?"*

"Sure, go ahead," Emilia said, as Luciana nodded.

The new girl sat beside Luciana. She picked up a spoon with her left hand and took a bite of her farofa. *"What did you guys think of the morning speeches?"*

"Ehhhh," Luciana shrugged. *"They were all boring."*

"Except for Snowbelle's!" Emilia put in. *"She's funny!"*

Luciana giggled. *"You're right! The way she talked about tripping over her ice slide the first time she summoned it was great!"*

"I'd definitely listen to another speech of hers," Emilia declared.

"Me, too." Luciana grinned.

"I thought Namikaze Tateru's was kind of interesting," the new girl put in.

"Oh yeah, the Japanese one?" Luciana said vaguely.

"That speech was weird," Emilia said, wrinkling her nose. *"If you ask me, she's big-time exaggerating. I mean, come on . . . regular memory wipes whenever they come back from a mission? That's practically brainwashing! Nobody would stand for it!"*

"Oh, I dunno," Luciana said, shrugging. *"It fits with the rumors I've heard about the* tianlong *who conquered Mongolia. China does it for national security reasons. And I'm pretty sure the* kamikaze *are worse. Like, didn't they conquer Russia or something?"*

"It was India," Emilia said.

"Korea?" the new girl suggested.

"Wait, I think it was Thailand," Emilia said. *"Or maybe it was the Philippines."*

"No, that's right, it was Korea!" Luciana exclaimed. *"Somebody mentioned that today!"*

"You mean like what Chung-Ae's ambassador was saying?" the new girl asked.

"That Korean who used big words?" Luciana wrinkled her nose. *"Oh, her speech was boring. I slept through the whole thing."*

Emilia giggled. *"Next time, play Tic Tac Toe with me and my friends! Wanna sit with me in the second half?"*

"Ha ha!" Luciana laughed. *"I'm not too worried. I think they saved all the most interesting speeches for the second half. Next up is Dulcina."*

"Oh, she's my hero!" Emilia squealed. *"She protects homeless kids and takes down the evil rich!"*

"And La Rama Fragrante's up after that. She's amazing."

"I know! Her healing powers have singlehandedly made Argentina's hospitals the best on the continent!"

"I've heard good things about Tat'yana Tsvetok."

"Didn't you hear the announcement? She was supposed to be in the first half, but she got replaced with Princesa at the last minute."

"No waaaaaay," Luciana moaned. *"Princesa's the worst. She's so stuck-up."*

"Yeah. At least the last speech was Snowbelle's, and she was fun."

"Well, Delicate Frost Princess might be fun, too. I mean, she was Snowbelle-trained."

"Yeah, but so is practically every girl in Antarctica. Hey, didn't you feel bad for Météore? She couldn't speak three words without stuttering!"

"Aww, yeah! I'm glad her translator understood what she was saying!" Turning to the new girl, Luciana added, *"Hey, what did you think —"*

She stopped abruptly.

"... Huh? She's missing."

Try as they might, neither Luciana nor Emilia could figure out when the other girl had left the conversation.

Chin-Sun walked down the hallway, her lips set in a thin line.

That conversation had confirmed what many other chattering girls had said during this lunch break.

Chin-Sun had not, of course, given up spying just because she was currently among allies. In fact, spying in friendly territory that you wanted to make sure *stayed* friendly was perhaps the most rewarding spying of all. The danger if discovered was lower, the caution was laxer, and the information gained was often richer.

Besides, infiltrating conversations between random audience members here gave her the opportunity to practice Portuguese and Spanish as well as English, which was a welcome change. Back home, she usually only had opportunities to speak Korean and Japanese, with occasional bouts of Mandarin if checking on the *tianlong*.

Chin-Sun loved languages, which was why she spoke twelve of them, and several dialects of each. She was currently studying Hungarian, since Chin-Sun might eventually want to listen in on a private conversation between Fecskefarkú Lepke and some other girl from Hungary. After that, she would probably start studying Arabic, in case of the same situation with Asiyah Azhaar.

She regretted that Tat'yana Tsvetok had backed out of the Union, because she'd hoped for opportunities to use her fluent Russian to spy on her.

Unlike Mun-Hee back in the Righteous Army, Chin-Sun didn't use magic to study languages, and she sneered at anyone who did. Becoming fluent in a foreign language wasn't really *that* difficult, so it seemed like sheer laziness to her. Not to mention that magic would disappear eventually, while anything you put in your head stayed there forever.

Chin-Sun was precise, hard-working, and effective. What she wasn't was very imaginative.

Perhaps the most obvious representation of this was the form her magical girl life took. Or rather, the lack of a regular form.

Chin-Sun was a shapeshifting magical girl.

Mild shapeshifting powers weren't uncommon, especially among magical girls who were part of the entertainment industry. Either a mild separation power, a mild shapeshifting power, or a mild illusion power was essential to make costume changes, so most magical girl actresses had one of the three.

Fighting magical girls with shapeshifting powers were unusual, but there were generally some around. Back in Korea, they had a girl in the Righteous Army with separate attack and defense forms, another whose costume changed colors depending on her mood, and a fellow *uileon sonyeo* spy had three different magical girl forms: one that appeared Japanese, one that appeared Chinese, and one that appeared Russian.

Pure shapeshifters were rare, though. Unless a specific look was decided upon before transforming originally, a magical girl form tended to reflect whatever a girl thought of as the ideal. So, in order to be a magical girl with no fixed form of your own, you pretty much either needed to have no body issues at all, or loads and loads of them.

Chin-Sun fell into the former category.

Some pure shapeshifting magical girls in the past had had very odd powers, such as transforming into microscopic organisms (a girl who'd volunteered at a medical laboratory), inanimate objects (later in life, that girl had gone into engineering), or mascots (given Golden Tingle Spray's apparent obsession with the uninvited animal-like creatures from other worlds, Chin-Sun was mildly surprised that she didn't have a power like that).

Chin-Sun had a much more standard shapeshifting power. Any human within about a mile radius she could imitate exactly, from face to voice to clothing. Unfortunately, this had an inconvenient limitation that meant she needed to plan carefully: if the person she was imitating decided to change clothes, take a shower, pull on a coat, or otherwise affect what they were wearing, Chin-Sun's transformation would automatically do the same, whether or not she was making the same gestures, which could be a dead giveaway that she was an imitator.

This was why she usually only imitated magical girl forms, since clothing tended to not change except during a power-up. Of course, this came with the risk that the girl might detransform suddenly, but it was better than the risk of what might happen if Chin-Sun was imitating a human who decided to use the bathroom.

She had been through that before. Never again.

Conversations chattered around Chin-Sun as she ambled down the hallway, picking up bits and pieces and adding them to her current analysis of the opinions of the crowd members here.

"No, Namikaze Tateru was right! You can tell there's a problem in Japan by looking at their average age of magical girl burnout there. I mean, ten and a half? That's two years younger than the worldwide average!"

"Oh, please. By that logic, you must think Mali is the most virtuous country in the world, with their average burnout age of fifteen, and the fact that they have thirty-year-old magical girls running around."

"Who's to say Mali *isn't* the most virtuous country in the world? Maybe they are."

"Oh, c'mon! It's not a world power or anything!"

In her head, still keeping an ear open for anything surprising she might overhear, Chin-Sun began composing a letter to Chung-Ae. She would put the report on paper later.

Our first speech of the morning speeches was from Princesa, the replacement for Tat'yana Tsvetok. She does not strike me as a good choice to have included in the Union. She is both a born mage and a magical girl, and gets highly defensive about her born mage power, which tends to annoy even those who wouldn't otherwise care. So nobody really trusts Princesa. This includes me.

It really was a shame that Tat'yana Tsvetok had backed out of the Union. It was even more unfortunate that Chin-Sun had so far been unable to unearth the reason why.

After her was Snowbelle, who has an oddly aggressive stance against using magic for fighting. She seems to think that magic should be used only for public service and self-expression, and claims fighting is a perversion of that. It is an attitude that strikes me as a luxury for those blessed to live in a nation without hostile neighbors, especially when there is also too high a concentration of magical girls for villains to attack frequently.

Chin-Sun had no fond feelings towards the Antarctican girl, who continued to treat Chin-Sun's aloof silences with indignant chatter.

Météore thinks we need to focus more on education. She made many excellent points, but I fear that no one paid attention to them because of her persistent stammer. I cannot object to her being here, but I suspect that she may be useless and ignored entirely by all the other, stronger personalities surrounding her.

This was a particular shame because Chin-Sun thought the issue was more important than the shy French girl even realized. More than once in her time wandering through *kamikaze* bases, Chin-Sun had noticed that those girls seemed to be chronically unaware of the consequences their powers might have. Education would go a long way towards fixing that.

Stopping the regular memory wipes might help, too.

Xinghuo believes in the tianlong's *"mandate of heaven" to turn the whole of Asia into China.*

Chin-Sun shook her head in exasperation.

Xinghuo was an official representative of the *tianlong*. It was little wonder she agreed with everything the nation was doing, even though Tibet and Mongolia were little better off than Korea right now.

And speaking of which . . .

Chin-Sun took a deep breath, starting to compose the most important paragraph of the letter.

Namikaze Tateru has removed all doubt about her loyalties. She spoke against the kamikaze, *decrying the way it has affected Japanese culture and families. She also spoke against Emperor Kami personally, saying that he is evil and insane. There is no doubt that Emperor Kami will be out for her life now.*

There was also no doubt that Florence Atkins and Eloise Santos had not approved that speech before it was given. They had sat on the stage with thunderstruck looks on their faces.

Of course, they must have understood that allowing a Japanese renegade into the Union, after the emperor had refused to send an official representative, was a slap in the face to the Japanese emperor. If they hadn't been willing to offend him, they would never have asked for the support of Chung-Ae and the Righteous Army in the first place. But . . .

Well, perhaps they hadn't expected Namikaze Tateru to make such a direct and open challenge.

Chin-Sun had to admit, she was impressed.

It may be that she is a potential ally, but we should be wary, Chin-Sun continued. *It is possible that her renegade status is only a ruse to earn our trust and destroy us. She was once a ranking member of the* kamikaze, *one of their most dangerous assets, and we do not know why that changed.*

As a *kamikaze,* her name had been "Namikaze Taterunai," which meant "don't make waves." After her sudden and violent rebellion, she had renamed herself exactly the opposite.

Nobody knew why she had done it, which meant it could have been a planned ruse.

But it also could have been genuine.

I am not sure if she would be a good ally or a volatile danger to us, as her primary concern is the way the magical girls in Japan are treated, and I am not sure if she agrees with what has been done to Korea, just not the methods for doing it. I have previously avoided speaking with her for that reason. Should I make overtures to see if we have a common goal that can be mutually advantageous? Please advise.

Chin-Sun went over that paragraph in her head again, making sure she was satisfied with it. Then she nodded shortly and moved on to the next speech in chronological order.

Edelweiss thinks we should be holding meetings in Germany, since it is the traditional center of the magic system. This was because Sunny, the first magical girl, had lived in Hamburg. *It is a pointless argument, so she wasted her speech on something that will make no difference. I think perhaps that she had little to say, however, seeing as her role is mainly to perform at concerts.*

Unlike the fifteen other girls on the Magical Girl Union's board of directors, Edelweiss never showed up at scheduled meetings, shirked any duties handed to her, and ignored Florence's panicked remonstrations. Chin-Sun suspected the only reason she hadn't been kicked out was that she kept giving concerts for fundraisers, and her name drew people to the Union.

Asiyah Azhaar believes the baree'a *need more representation.* That was the Arabic term for magical girls, a word referring to their innocence. *I believe she feels uncomfortable that Tat'yana Tsvetok has left, and she wants another pacifist to join. She has recommended friends of hers from Qatar, Kuwait, and Palestine. I do not think a quiet pacifist can be useful to us, but if you think there would be any purpose in doing so, I would be willing to see if there is some way I can sway Florence to invite another* baree'a *into the Union.*

The next two speeches made Chin-Sun snort in remembrance. They had been polar opposites, and the first girl had shot poisonous glances at the second girl all through the second girl's speech.

Jeanne d'Rouen wants fewer mascots pleading favors. Golden Tingle Spray wants more help for mascot-aiders. I think there is a large tension brewing there.

Chin-Sun had nothing more to say on that topic, as she had no interest in the outcome of that fight.

With chagrin, she took a deep breath and began to compose her final paragraph.

Alas, I fear I must report that my speech was not a success. My recitation of our most troubling statistics failed to fulfill the intended purpose of stirring the hearts of those listening. Nobody really listened to my speech, and many people have reported it was boring. Perhaps it would have been better to . . .

A girl wearing a fluffy pink dress turned the corner ahead of Chin-Sun and stopped abruptly.

"AAAAAAAAAA! Who are you?! Why do you look like me?!"

Chin-Sun was not very good at improvising, but she was terrific at following a rehearsed script. And she'd ended up in this situation many times before.

So she immediately clasped her hands together and squealed, *"Oh, wow! I'm your biggest fan! Can I have your autograph?!"*

The girl stared at her in bafflement. *"Uh . . . sure?"*

"Here's a piece of paper!" Chin-Sun cried, whipping a poster off the wall and shoving it over at her.

Looking mystified, the girl slowly signed it.

"Yaaaaaaaaaaaaaay!" Chin-Sun shrieked, snatching the poster and racing off excitedly down the hallway.

As soon as she was out of sight, she ducked behind a pillar and detransformed back into herself.

It's depressing how often that works, Chin-Sun thought, shaking her head. She, of course, had no clue who that girl had been. She had picked a member of the audience at random. But vanity rarely failed to give her enough time to escape.

"Oh, so that's your power," a voice in Japanese said.

Chin-Sun stiffened and spun around to see Namikaze Tateru standing behind her. There had been no sign of anyone nearby, and Chin-Sun was good at knowing when she was being watched, so clearly the girl had some sort of stealth power.

She said nothing, standing there warily.

"I've wondered about you," the dangerous renegade said casually, ambling over. Her shoulder-length straight black hair remained still, not stirring a breath as she walked. Only a magical girl form could do that. *"You never transform in front of us or mention your powers. You barely talk at all, in fact — just do your assignments and listen to everybody. It reminds me of myself when I was thinking of betraying the* kamikaze.*"*

Chin-Sun stared at her with no expression.

"Well," Namikaze Tateru said, *"I'm no fan of our emperor, in case you hadn't noticed. He's a tyrant, and I'd waste no tears if somebody assassinated him."*

She stopped and waited expectantly.

Chin-Sun said nothing. She would make no deals without Chung-Ae's approval.

"Okay. We'll talk later, then."

Namikaze Tateru vanished in a wave of cherry blossoms, which vanished themselves a moment later.

Either teleportation or illusion, Chin-Sun noted. *I will guess illusion that she guises as teleportation, because that would work as part of a stealth power.*

Namikaze Taterunai, the *kamikaze,* had had power over oceans and waves. It seemed that Namikaze Tateru had different magic.

That did lend a slight credence to the idea that her defection from the *kamikaze* was real.

Chin-Sun took a deep breath and added a new paragraph to the letter to Chung-Ae in her head.

Namikaze Tateru has figured out what my magic is. She seems to want to start negotiations with us. I am not sure if she's trustworthy. Should I talk with her, or would you rather send a different ambassador or have me avoid her altogether? Please advise.

Sometimes Chin-Sun wished that every girl in the Union could be as unsuspecting as Snowbelle and Florence, who had left Chin-Sun alone on the airplane to go through their things while they'd gone to recruit Dulcina.

Still . . . if Namikaze Tateru hadn't been suspicious, she would probably never have left the *kamikaze*.

Assuming she had.

With a sigh, Chin-Sun headed back to her room to write the letter down.

Chapter 4
The Impasse

Zoning out from exhaustion and stress, Florence nearly missed the last line of Eloise Santos's closing speech.

"...wraps up the opening ceremonies, everyone," Eloise Santos was saying in English, having already stated what Florence assumed was the same thing in Portuguese. "Thank you for attending!"

The audience got up and started to chatter, a roar filling the large assembly hall.

Florence breathed a sigh of relief, eager to stretch her legs. She'd been sitting stiffly up on this stage for hours, afraid to so much as scratch her nose, lest it invite somebody's censure.

"Florence. A word in private?" Presidente Santos murmured, striding past her.

Florence's blood went chill. She knew what that meant. The president of Mágico always praised in public and criticized in private.

"Um..."

She suddenly wanted to stay glued to her seat.

But she got up, of course, and reluctantly followed the woman off the stage, past armed security guards, past the two more layers of magical girl security guards, and into the private hallway that led to the presidential suite.

The Impasse

As soon as they were walking through the hallway lined with pillars, away from any overhearing ears, the president looked back at her and said, "I asked you to discuss your new magical girl form in your presentation. You did not do this."

"How could I?" Florence said defensively. "I don't know what it is myself yet!"

Eloise Santos paused. "You . . ."

Uh oh. Florence cringed.

"You *haven't chosen it yet?*" Eloise Santos exploded. "I asked you to make that a *priority!*"

"I know!" Florence said hastily. "I just haven't had any good ideas! And I've been so busy with organizing the ceremonies and planning my speech —"

— and doing all of Edelweiss's work, even though you told me to just fire her and put somebody else in her place, and homework, which you told me to stop wasting my time on, and freaking out about the possible futures of the Union, which I don't want to tell you about because telling anybody about any of them might make them more likely —

"Florence," the president said flatly. "No one appreciates a leader who is wishy-washy. You can be a former magical girl. You can be a current magical girl. But you *can't* just keep hovering."

Florence gulped. "I know. It's just . . . I need more time . . ."

"Time is a luxury, not a guarantee, Florence," the woman said in an irate tone. "Make. It. A. Priority."

Without another word, Eloise Santos reached the door of her private suite and opened it, entered, and slammed it behind her.

Florence swallowed and held her arm. *I'm trying . . .*

It wasn't that she didn't care about her future magical girl form. She did. But self-analysis just wasn't something she'd had much time for over the past few months. There had always been somebody who needed her attention, something urgent that had to be done, and recently, some new terror to worry about.

It just wasn't that easy to make up your mind about what path you wanted your entire future to take. She'd done it before, of course, but . . .

But I didn't have to figure it out all by myself the first time, Florence thought moodily. *Kendra's mother had sketches for us to go through, and Kendra was being so pushy to try to make me match her costume that I figured out what I wanted practically out of self-defense.*

As long as everyone was pressuring her to make a decision, part of Florence rebelled and absolutely refused to perform to their idea of when the timing of her choice ought to be.

I never used to make decisions like this alone, Florence admitted reluctantly to herself. *Kendra always helped me figure out what to do. If it was a good idea, I'd go along with it. If it was a bad idea, we'd fight over it until I'd figure out why I hated it, and that would help me figure out what kind of plan I did want.*

Even when we disagreed . . .

She winced, remembering a few of their worst fights.

. . . which may have happened more frequently than I like to think . . .

Kendra hadn't responded all that well to Florence's choice of boyfriend, or Florence's change of hairstyle, or Florence's choice of magical girl form in the first place. Which had made her feel like she had definitely done the right thing, in all three cases.

But . . . in at least one of those cases, it had been a disastrous mistake. Thinking about the horrible choice she'd made to date Lute Deathwave still made Florence feel sick to her stomach.

What if . . . what if Kendra driving me to make a decision quickly wasn't always a good thing?

What if sometimes Florence had made the wrong choice, just because it wasn't a different wrong choice Kendra was trying to shove down her throat?

What if Florence had gotten so used to reacting to Kendra that she'd lost the ability to make choices all on her own?

What if her dependence on Kendra was the reason the original nightmare future had happened in the first place?

What if everything was Florence's fault?

It ate away at Florence to remember that she would have been useless in the future that Kendra had turned villain to prevent.

The Impasse

"You were my second-in-command, and you weren't capable of stopping me, or anyone else in the Union, for that matter," Kendra had said, sneeringly.

Would Florence really have been that pathetic? That helpless?

Would she really have not tried to stop her?

The more she thought about it, the more angry she was with herself.

What kind of best friend wouldn't stop her best friend from becoming a dangerous demagogue?

What had she been *doing* in that future? Sitting around, hemming and hawing undecidedly?

Well, no more! She would be decisive! And she'd do it without a moment of Kendra's input, thanks very much!

Florence squared her shoulders, marched forward, and knocked on the president's door.

It opened, and the president stood there with an impatient air, her hair half taken down from the wing-shaped hairclips she'd been wearing.

Florence took a deep breath. "Celestial Dragon. My new magical girl name will be Celestial Dragon."

"No," the president said.

"The bracelet has twelve stones, so I'm thinking I'll have twelve different powers —" Florence stalled to a halt. "What?"

"No, you can't use that name. 'Celestial Dragon' is what *tianlong* translates to. It'll imply blatant favoritism towards China, and that's the last thing we need after the stunt Namikaze Tateru pulled today. I'm already going to have to send a letter of apology to Japan, saying that her views don't reflect the views of Mágico."

"But —" Florence objected. "But it fits! I've always had a dragon theme, and I care about heaven —"

"You can't use 'Celestial Dragon,'" Eloise Santos said flatly. "Choose something else."

Then she shut the door.

Florence's shoulders drooped, and she fought back tears. First the woman had told her to hurry up and choose, and now she was telling her the name she'd picked wasn't good enough.

Was Florence really in charge of the Union?

Was Kendra's absence really going to make a difference?

Would any of Florence's choices ever matter at all?

Kendra held one of the dueling magical girls in a chokehold with one arm while she brandished her spiked halo at the other.

Both of the contentious girls looked panicked, and the one in the chokehold was gasping for breath.

"You know why I've been able to defeat you?" Kendra snarled. "Because you were fighting one another. That makes you *weak!*"

"Sh-she's right," the girl in the chokehold gasped tearfully. "I'm sorry for stealing your boyfriend, Angie."

"I'm sorry for filling your swimming pool with green goo," the other girl sniffled.

"I'm sorry I buried the TV remote."

"I'm sorry I shredded your prom dress."

"I'm sorry I put the toaster in your shower."

"I'm sorry I — *YOU BURIED THE TV REMOTE?!*"

"Waaah! I'm sorry!"

Good, Kendra thought, rolling her eyes, letting the two girls escape. *Now they can stop being so stupid, and . . .*

"Angela!" one girl cried, touching her palms to her friend's.

"Celeste!" her friend gasped, doing the same.

"Let's renew our friendship by . . ."

The girls spun around and summoned a pair of wands.

"*. . . defeating this villain together!*"

Kendra burst into a panicked run, reaching into her belt for the watch as a deadly corkscrew of bubbles and stars burst from their wands and lanced after her.

Aaaaaaaaaaaaaarrrrrrrrgggghhhhhh!!!

As she sprinted, she seized the watch and teleported back to the lair, slamming into a wall.

WHAM!

"Welcome back, Kendra," Chronos said without looking up from her crocheting. "Let me guess how they redefined their friendship."

The Impasse

Kendra picked herself up from the floor, checked to make sure her nose was still intact, and glowered. "Not . . . one . . . word."

"About the warning you wouldn't listen to?" Chronos asked innocently. "Wouldn't dream of it."

"Well, at least I tried to fix it, and *succeeded!*" Kendra snarled. "That's more than *you've* ever done! You sit there all superior as if you know better, but you've never been out on a battlefield in your life!"

And with that, she stormed up the stairs to her bedroom, as extra-loudly as possible.

It didn't quite drown out the sound of her teammate and the useless brat down below.

"Kendra sure is grumpy lately, isn't she?" Tiffany commented, hammering yet another poster of stuffed animals and smiling sunshines onto the wall, rather than using a thumbtack.

"Just 'lately'?" Chronos muttered, rolling her eyes. "But yes. I'm not sure how much longer we can keep this stalemate."